UNICORN ACADEMY
NATURE MAGIC

For a moment, Feather was silent. Then she asked quietly, "Do you think I can do this, Lily? Do you really believe my magic is strong enough?"

Lily didn't hesitate. "Yes. I do. You can help save the school, Feather. I know it."

★ ★ ★

LOOK OUT FOR MORE ADVENTURES WITH

UNICORN ACADEMY
NATURE MAGIC

Lily and Feather

Phoebe and Shimmer

Zara and Moonbeam

Aisha and Silver

★ ★ ★

UNICORN ACADEMY

NATURE MAGIC 1

Lily and Feather

JULIE SYKES
illustrated by LUCY TRUMAN

A STEPPING STONE BOOK™

Random House 🏠 New York

Text copyright © 2020 by Julie Sykes and Linda Chapman
Cover art and interior illustrations copyright © 2020 by Lucy Truman

All rights reserved. Published in the United States by Random House Children's
Books, a division of Penguin Random House LLC, New York.
Originally published in paperback in the United Kingdom by
Nosy Crow Ltd, London, in 2020.

Random House and the colophon are registered trademarks and
A Stepping Stone Book and the colophon are trademarks of
Penguin Random House LLC.

Visit us on the Web! rhcbooks.com

Educators and librarians, for a variety of teaching tools, visit us at
RHTeachersLibrarians.com

Library of Congress Cataloging-in-Publication Data
Names: Sykes, Julie, author. | Truman, Lucy, illustrator.
Title: Lily and Feather / Julie Sykes ; illustrated by Lucy Truman.
Description: First American edition. | New York : Random House
Children's Books, [2021] | Series: Unicorn Academy Nature Magic ; 1 |
"A Stepping Stone book." | Audience: Ages 6-9. | Summary: Lily and her
unicorn, Feather, are eager to make friends and learn to be guardians of
Unicorn Island, but will they be able to stop the strange tornadoes
threatening Unicorn Academy and its students?
Identifiers: LCCN 2020050447 (print) | LCCN 2020050448 (ebook) |
ISBN 978-0-593-42669-2 (paperback) | ISBN 978-0-593-42670-8 (lib. bdg.) |
ISBN 978-0-593-42671-5 (ebook)
Subjects: CYAC: Unicorns—Fiction. |
Magic—Fiction. | Friendship—Fiction. | Boarding schools—Fiction. |
Schools—Fiction.
Classification: LCC PZ7.S98325 Lf 2021 (print) |
LCC PZ7.S98325 (ebook) | DDC [E]—dc23

Printed in the United States of America
10 9 8 7 6 5 4 3 2 1
First American Edition

To the Quornicorns Pony Club Quiz Team—
Cleo, Mia, Libby, and Iola—
you are all absolute stars!

CHAPTER 1

"Here we are, Lils," Lily's mom said. "Unicorn Academy—your home for the next year!"

"Oh, wow!" Lily's breath rushed out as she stared up at the enormous glass-and-marble building. On the top of the tallest tower, a pink flag with a white unicorn on it was rippling in the breeze. "It's beautiful," she said. She looked at the gardens full of winter plants and flowers, and the lake shimmering in the distance.

Her mother smiled. "It is, isn't it? It hasn't changed one bit since I was here. You're going to have such a fantastic time. I just know it!"

Lily couldn't speak. Her stomach felt like it was tying itself in knots. She'd wanted to come to Unicorn Academy for ages—she couldn't wait to be paired with a unicorn and start training to become a guardian of beautiful Unicorn Island. However, now that she was here and the academy looked so big, she was beginning to wonder whether her invitation to become a student had been a mistake. The other new students all looked so confident as they chatted with each other and waved goodbye to their parents.

What if I'm not good enough to be a guardian? Lily thought with a rush of panic. *What if I mess things up and get asked to leave? Mom will be so disappointed.*

A teacher walked up. She wore her brown hair in a neat bun held in place with silver clips. Three girls were following her.

"Hello, I'm Ms. Rosemary. I teach Care of Unicorns. And what's your name?" the teacher said to Lily.

Lily was feeling so overwhelmed, the words seemed to stick in her throat. "I'm . . . um . . . um . . . ," she stammered.

"Lily Jamieson," her mom offered.

Ms. Rosemary looked at her clipboard. "That's lucky! Lily, you're going to be in Amethyst dorm with these three. This is Aisha." She pointed to a girl who was carrying a flute case and had curly black hair in a high ponytail. The girl grinned at Lily, who smiled shyly back.

"And this is Zara," Ms. Rosemary continued. Zara had dark brown hair that stopped just past her shoulders and green eyes. She studied Lily for a moment and then gave her a smile.

"And Phoebe," Ms. Rosemary finished. Phoebe

was tall and slim, with honey-blond hair in two waist-length braids. She grinned.

"Hi, Lily! Isn't this super awesome!" She swept her arms out. "I mean, look around. It's gorgeous, isn't it? We're just so lucky to have been invited to be students here!"

Lily thought it sounded like everything Phoebe said had an exclamation mark after it.

"Say goodbye to your mom, Lily," said Ms. Rosemary. "Then we need to get to the hall. It's almost time for the ceremony where you will be paired with your unicorns."

Lily felt a flutter of delight. She was going to have a unicorn of her own!

Mom stepped forward. "Goodbye, Lils. Have a wonderful time. Make sure you write and tell me all your news." She hugged her and then gently pushed her toward Ms. Rosemary. "Go on, off you go!"

Torn between excitement at meeting her unicorn and sadness at saying goodbye to her

mom, and still feeling like she'd been invited to the academy by mistake, Lily followed Ms. Rosemary and the other girls up the marble steps and through the front door into the academy. The entrance hall was large, with statues of unicorns in the corners and huge oil paintings on the walls.

"No more talking, please," Ms. Rosemary said with a warning look at Phoebe, who was saying something to Zara.

As Ms. Rosemary led them all into the main hall, Lily swallowed a gasp. Light shone through the colored swirls of the domed glass roof, filling the hall with rainbows and shining on a huge map that was in the center of the room. Lily stood on her tiptoes for a better look. The magical force field that kept the map safe hummed softly as she passed by. Lily's mom had told her it was an exact model of Unicorn Island and it could transport anyone anywhere on the island. Students and

unicorns were not allowed to use it without Ms. Nettles's permission. Lily hoped she'd get to use it at some point.

That's if I'm good enough to stay here, she reminded herself.

"Oh, wow! Look at the unicorns!" Aisha whispered, pointing.

A fresh wave of excitement swept away Lily's anxiety as she followed Aisha's gaze and saw a group of young unicorns standing at the side of the stage. They were beautiful. Their sparkling white coats were covered with different-colored patterns, and their long silky manes and tails were full of colors. Some of them eyed the students boldly, but others hung back, peeping out shyly from behind the stage curtains.

"Lily, over here!" Hearing her name, Lily saw that Aisha, Phoebe, and Zara had gone on ahead and were now waving her over to a row of seats.

But just as Lily stepped toward them, two other girls barged past. One had bushy brown hair and narrow eyes, and the other had red hair in a high ponytail. "Come on, Amber. Let's sit here!" said the brown-haired girl. They sat in the seats next to Aisha, Phoebe, and Zara.

"Excuse me, but Lily was about to sit there," said Zara politely.

The two girls raised their eyebrows.

"It's okay. I'll sit somewhere else," said Lily quickly. The girls looked scary.

"Oh, please, can't you both sit somewhere else? We'd really like to sit together because we're in the same dorm," Aisha said to the two girls.

"Tough," said the brown-haired girl with a shrug.

"It's fine," Lily said. "I can sit back there." She pointed to a seat in the row behind them.

The brown-haired girl nudged her friend, the girl she had called Amber. "Did you hear her squeak?"

"Yeah, she sounds like a little mouse, doesn't she, Skye?" Amber snickered.

"A teeny-tiny mouse," Skye giggled.

Lily hid behind a wing of her hair as she dived into the row of seats behind them. She was very glad Skye and Amber weren't in her dorm. They seemed horrible!

Just then, Ms. Nettles, the tall head teacher, walked out onto the stage and clapped her hands. She had a long nose with tiny glasses balanced on the end of it.

Silence quickly fell.

"Welcome to Unicorn Academy," Ms. Nettles said. "Over the course of this year, you will train and bond with your own special unicorn. You and your unicorn will be partners for life, helping each other and looking after Unicorn Island. You will graduate at the end of the year, after your unicorn has discovered their magic and you have bonded with them. You will know when this happens, as a lock of your hair will turn the same color as your unicorn's mane. Some unicorns need a little longer to discover their magic, or to bond, so some of you may need to stay for a second year in order to graduate."

Ms. Nettles seemed to glance in Lily's direction. Lily squirmed in her seat. Did the head teacher think she might not graduate? To her relief, Ms. Nettles's gaze swept on.

"You will make many friends while you are here, but the most important friendship will be the one you form with your unicorn. In December, on the longest night of the year,

students and their unicorns will graduate at the Sparkle Lake Ball! Then you will return home together as lifelong friends and partners.

"But to start this exciting journey, you must first be paired with a unicorn." A smile softened her strict face. "Let the pairing ceremony begin!"

CHAPTER 2

Lily studied the unicorns eagerly. Which one would be hers? Hopefully not the tall unicorn with the silver-blue mane and proud stare. He was very beautiful but looked far too regal to be her partner. She wouldn't know what to say to him! And the smaller unicorn next to him with the red-and-orange mane looked too naughty and mischievous. A unicorn with a pretty pink mane shouldered past him and stamped a hoof, looking confidently out at the audience.

Lily's attention was caught by a unicorn with a violet-yellow-and-blue mane who was standing at

the back. She was peeking out shyly from under her silky forelock. Her long eyelashes fluttered as she glanced out at the girls and boys before staring at the floor. Lily's heart melted. The unicorn looked awkward, as if she felt she didn't belong there. *Just like me,* Lily thought.

Ms. Nettles began to call out names—the student's first and then the unicorn's. The first pairing was a boy from Topaz dorm called Spike, who had bright red hair and a sly smile, and Dynamo, the mischievous unicorn with the red-and-orange mane. They both seemed delighted as they moved to the far side of the stage, immediately putting their matching red

heads together and looking as though they were planning to cause trouble.

One by one, Ms. Nettles called out names until it was Amethyst dorm's turn.

"Aisha," said Ms. Nettles. "You will be paired with Silver."

Aisha shimmied from her chair, humming a happy tune. Silver was a small unicorn with a green-silver-and-red mane. He danced out from the crowd, lifting his glittering hooves high, his tail swishing. Aisha ran up the steps and threw her arms around him. He nuzzled her happily, and hearing the sound of her tune, he trotted in time to it as they walked over to the far side of the stage.

The watching students giggled.

"Oh dear," said Ms. Nettles, shaking her head. "I hope I haven't made a mistake pairing you two music lovers together!" She silenced the gigglers

with a stern look. "Next from Amethyst dorm we have Phoebe. You will be paired with Shimmer."

Phoebe gave a high-pitched squeal of delight as a unicorn with a long pink-and-blue mane whinnied. "Oh, wow! I was hoping for that exact unicorn! Thank you, Ms. Nettles! Thank you! You've made my dreams come true!" She ran up the steps and hugged the head teacher, who looked very taken aback.

"That will do, my dear!" she said, shooing Phoebe away.

"This is the best day of my ENTIRE life, everyone!" Phoebe said. She raced over to Shimmer.

"We will be friends forever!" Shimmer exclaimed with a toss of his mane. He seemed just as dramatic as Phoebe.

Ms. Nettles cleared her throat. "Very nice, dears. Now move to the side, please."

Phoebe and Shimmer left the center of the stage and joined Aisha and Silver.

Zara was paired with a dreamy-looking unicorn with a pure silver mane, called Moonbeam, and then finally it was Lily's turn.

"Lily, you will be paired with . . ."

Lily's heart raced as she stared at the remaining unicorns. Which one was it going to be?

"Feather," Ms. Nettles announced.

Lily's heart leaped as the nervous unicorn she'd spotted earlier stepped forward. Feather stumbled awkwardly as she reached the center of the stage. Lily hurried up the steps, blushing, aware that the whole room was watching them.

"Um . . . hi," she said.

"Hi," muttered Feather, staring at the floor.

Lily could tell Feather hated being watched by everyone just as much as she did. It made her feel braver, like she wanted to protect her.

"I was hoping you'd be my unicorn," she whispered.

Feather's eyes flew to hers, and as their gazes met, Lily felt a strong connection surge between them. Feather nuzzled her, her warm, sweet-smelling breath tickling Lily's hands.

They joined the others in Amethyst dorm while Ms. Nettles moved on to Opal dorm. All around Lily, the students who had been paired up were whispering excitedly to their unicorns. She and Feather exchanged shy looks.

Skye and Amber, the two girls who had been mean to Lily, were in Opal dorm and were the last to be matched with their unicorns.

Skye was given a sweet-looking unicorn called Firefly, and Amber was paired with Swift, the impatient unicorn with the pink mane. The noise level rose.

Ms. Nettles clapped her hands for silence. "You now have the rest of the afternoon to get to know your unicorn. Make the most of this free time. Lessons will start tomorrow. Schedules will be in your bedroom when you go to unpack."

"Where would you like to go first?" Lily asked

Feather as they all filed out the back door of the hall.

"I don't mind," Feather whispered.

"I don't mind, either," said Lily.

Skye and Amber were passing by.

"I don't mind. I don't mind, either," mimicked Skye, perfectly copying Feather's and Lily's voices.

Amber giggled. "Listen, Skye, Lily's squeaking like a tiny mouse again."

Feather glared at them.

"What are you doing here?" Skye said, looking Lily up and down. "You're such a little mouse. The teachers must have made a mistake inviting you to train at Unicorn Academy."

Lily's heart clenched and her eyes glistened with tears as Skye spoke her greatest fear. Luckily, Skye was already looking around for the next thing to do and didn't notice. "Come on, Amber, let's find our dorm and go exploring!"

she said, climbing onto Firefly and trotting away.

Amber leaped onto Swift and cantered after her.

Lily blinked, trying hard not to cry.

Feather nuzzled her. "I don't like that girl. She's mean."

Lily felt a little better.

"Hey, Lily!"

Hearing Zara's voice, Lily swung around. The rest of her dorm was beckoning her over. "We thought we'd ride around the grounds together so we can get to know each other as we explore," said Zara. "Do you and Feather want to join us?"

What Lily really wanted was to go somewhere on her own with Feather, but she didn't want her dorm to think she was unfriendly. She swallowed the hard lump in her throat. "Okay. Thanks," she managed to say, and jumping onto Feather, she joined the others.

✦ ★ ✦ ★

"We should dip our hands in Sparkle Lake as we look around," said Aisha. "My dad said it's a tradition on your first day here."

Lily's mom had told her that too. She was just about to tell the others that but she was too late—Zara had started talking.

"Did you know that all the magic water that flows around the island comes from Sparkle Lake? It rises up from the center of the earth through the fountain in the middle of the lake, and then it's carried around the island in rivers and streams."

"I really want to see it!" said Phoebe.

"Then what are we waiting for?" said Zara. "Let's go!"

As Lily explored with the others, she tried to push Skye's words to the back of her mind. They rode to the glittering lake, to the play park, through the neat vegetable garden and orchard, then down to the stream that ran through the meadows.

I love it here, Lily thought, her heart filling with delight. *I want to learn how to protect the school and the island. I'm going to try really hard in all my lessons. Oh, please let Skye be wrong and let me be good enough to stay.*

They reached the cross-country course. Lily looked eagerly at it. She had a pony back home and she often took him jumping. She couldn't wait to take Feather jumping, but there was a sign posted saying they couldn't jump without a teacher. "I love cross-country," she said.

"Me too!" said Zara.

"Look at those jumps!" Phoebe squealed. "They're huge! Have you ever jumped fences like that?" She didn't wait for them to answer. "I did once. I was riding my sister's horse at home and he just took off and galloped toward an enormous hedge. I was so scared, but I managed to stay on."

"It looks like Topaz dorm has been here before us," Zara said, riding up to a big log pile. "Spike and Dynamo ignored the sign and jumped this fence."

Lily wondered how she could possibly know that. Phoebe clearly had the same thought. "How can you tell?" she asked.

"Look," said Zara. "There are four sets of hoofprints leading up to the jump. Topaz dorm is the only other dorm with four people in it, so it must have been them. There's only one set of hoofprints leading away from the jump and the hooves have an oval shape. I noticed that Dynamo's hooves were shaped like that when Spike was paired with him. The final clue, well, look over there!" She pointed to the jump.

Even Aisha had stopped humming to listen. "What are we looking at?" she asked.

"Don't you see the red and orange hairs caught

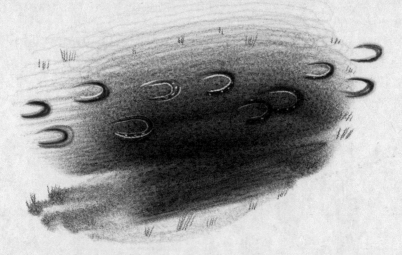

on the wood? They must have snagged there as a unicorn jumped." Zara rode Moonbeam over. "Dynamo is the only unicorn in Topaz dorm to have a red-and-orange mane, so it must have been him."

"That's so cool!" said Phoebe, her eyes wide.

"You're just like a detective, Zara!" agreed Aisha.

Lily nodded hard.

Zara grinned. "I love solving mysteries, and while I'm here at the academy I intend to solve any that come our way!"

Lily forced herself to speak. "My mom said that lots of mysterious things happened here last year."

"Yes, I heard that," said Zara. "Someone was trying to harm the unicorns."

"It was the old school nurse, Ms. Willow," said Phoebe. "She was trying to poison them all with one of her special tonics! Most of the unicorns almost died!"

"No, they didn't," said Zara. "Honestly, Phoebe, if you keep exaggerating and making stuff up, then no one will believe you when you are telling the truth. Ms. Willow never tried to poison anyone. She wanted to bind all the unicorns to her so that they had to do what she said. The year before that, the head teacher at that time—Ms. Primrose—turned bad and tried to ruin the whole school."

Aisha's eyes shone. "Oh, I hope something exciting happens while we're here. Imagine how much fun it would be to have a mystery to solve."

Lily grinned. It did sound exciting.

"We must keep our eyes peeled!" Phoebe declared. "If any mystery comes along, we'll work it out!"

"Definitely," said Zara. "Amethyst dorm is the best. We'll always save the day!"

The unicorns whinnied as the four new friends cheered.

CHAPTER 3

Lily's first few days at the academy flew by. There was so much to do—teachers to meet, stable routines to work out, names to learn, and lessons to start. Lily concentrated really hard in all her classes, not wanting to give the teachers any excuse to be unhappy with her. She didn't like putting her hand up in class because she hated it when everyone looked at her, but she tried to make up for being quiet by putting lots of effort into her work. She was so tired at the end of each day that she fell asleep the minute she got into bed.

"Can you believe we've been at the academy for three days?" she said to Feather on the fourth morning as she got her ready for their first lesson of the day—Care of Unicorns with Ms. Rosemary. Lily already thought of Feather as her best friend. She could talk to her about anything without feeling awkward or worrying about what Feather would think of her.

"It's gone really fast," Feather agreed. "But . . ."

"But what?' Lily prompted, lifting a strand of mane to comb it out.

"I really like it here, but I still don't really know the other unicorns very well. They all act like they've known each other forever."

"I feel like that too," Lily admitted. "Zara, Aisha, and Phoebe talk all the time, but I never know what to say so I usually don't say anything at all. I really like them, but I bet they all think I'm boring."

"No one could think that!" said Feather.

Lily smiled. "Thanks. I wish I could just speak out more . . ." She broke off as Phoebe, Zara, and Aisha arrived in the stables with a group of other students.

Phoebe pointed dramatically at Lily. "It's Lily! She's safe!"

Lily blinked. "What?"

Phoebe waved a crumpled piece of paper with Lily's name in the corner. "I found this in the dorm when we got up. You seemed to have disappeared. We were sure that you'd been kidnapped and you were trying to write us a note before you were taken away."

"Actually, it was *Phoebe* who was sure you'd been kidnapped," Zara put in with a sigh. "I was pretty sure you'd be here. You always get up early, before the rest of us. Your boots and coat had gone, and I noticed that you'd taken the roll of braiding ribbon that had been on your bedside table."

"So *is* this yours?" Phoebe held out the piece of paper to Lily.

"Yes, I meant to throw it away, but I must have missed," said Lily, stuffing the paper in a pocket. She loved folding paper into shapes, and she'd been trying to make a unicorn, but it hadn't gone very well.

"It was just a bit of scrap paper, like Zara said. You're such a drama queen, Phoebe," said Aisha, shaking her head.

"I might have been right," said Phoebe. "Lily might have been kidnapped."

"Lily? Kidnapped?" Skye scoffed to Amber as they walked past. "Who'd want to kidnap quiet little Lily Mouse! She'd bore her kidnappers to death!"

"Yeah," Amber agreed. "I bet the teachers

wouldn't even notice she was gone, she's so quiet."

They giggled together as they went to get their grooming kits.

Lily tipped her head forward so a wing of hair hid her embarrassment. The last thing she wanted was for Skye and Amber to look back and start squeaking at her. It was bad enough when they called her Lily Mouse.

"Ignore them," said Aisha, glaring after Skye and Amber.

Lily nodded. She knew that was the best thing to do, but it was easier said than done.

Ms. Rosemary arrived carrying a big box of colored ribbons. "Morning, everyone. As I told you yesterday, we're going to be practicing braiding today. I'm going to demonstrate on my unicorn, Blossom. Please make your way outside now with your unicorns and bring your grooming kits."

Lily and Feather stayed behind as everyone rushed to go outside, tagging along at the back as the students and unicorns formed a large circle around Blossom.

"Before you can start braiding, you need to comb your unicorn's mane out with either of these," said Ms. Rosemary, holding up a metal comb and a soft brush. "You start by sectioning the mane into small pieces, like this." As Ms. Rosemary began separating out Blossom's golden mane, Ms. Nettles appeared and beckoned her over.

The two teachers broke off to talk in whispers, glancing toward Lily and Feather.

"Lily, they seem to be looking at us," said Feather uneasily.

"I know." Lily felt anxious as she watched Ms. Rosemary and Ms. Nettles glance at them again. *Had Ms. Nettles realized she'd made a mistake in inviting her to train as a guardian? Had she heard how quiet she was in class? Was she going to send her home?* Her heart sped up as Ms. Nettles walked over.

Ms. Nettles smiled kindly. "Lily dear, I'd like to talk to you. It won't take long."

Lily could feel everyone's eyes on her as she followed Ms. Nettles over to a drinking trough in a quiet corner of the yard. Her heart was now banging like a drum.

Ms. Nettles turned to face her.

"Please don't send me home!" The words burst out of Lily before Ms. Nettles could speak. "Please,

Ms. Nettles! I really want to be a guardian. I don't want to leave! I'll try really hard to speak more."

Ms. Nettles blinked in surprise. "Leave? Whatever are you talking about, Lily?"

"I . . . I . . . ," Lily stuttered. "I thought you were about to say that you'd made a mistake by inviting me to be a student here."

Ms. Nettles's gaze softened. "I most certainly was not about to say that. Your teachers have all told me how pleased they are with you. They say you are one of our hardest-working students. Why ever would I want to send you home?"

Lily looked at the floor.

Ms. Nettles regarded her for a moment. "You are certainly not about to be sent home, and I definitely have not made a mistake. Guardians all have different strengths, just as unicorns have different magic powers. I hope you will discover your own strengths while you are here. Now, the

reason I need to talk to you is about your mother."

Lily felt a rush of anxiety. "Is she okay?"

"Yes. She phoned me this morning because she wanted you to know that she's moving in with your auntie Louise for a bit. There was a strange weather event last night, and your village was hit by a tornado. A purple one. It destroyed many of the buildings."

Lily's hands flew to her mouth. "Oh no! Was anyone hurt?"

Ms. Nettles shook her head. "Thankfully not. However, some of the houses, including your own, will need to be rebuilt. The tornado was very strong."

"That's awful!" said Lily. She sniffed, suddenly feeling

very homesick and wishing that she was back in her village so that she could check on everyone. "And really strange—we've never had a tornado in my village before." Her village was on the east coast of the island and protected by a range of mountains. It was very rare for them to have bad weather of any kind.

"It is extremely unusual," agreed Ms. Nettles. "Luckily, as I said, there were no injuries."

Lily nodded.

Feather's dark eyes were full of concern as Lily rejoined the lesson. "Is everything all right?"

In whispers, Lily told Feather what had happened.

Feather rubbed her head against Lily's arm. "How scary. Your poor mom. It sounds like she had a lucky escape."

"I know. I wish I could see her and give her a hug." Lily thought of the piece of crumpled

paper in her pocket. As soon as the lesson was over, she'd smooth out the paper and fold it into a dove, her mother's favorite bird, and send it to her.

Aisha, Zara, and Phoebe came over. "What did Ms. Nettles want?" Aisha whispered, glancing at Ms. Rosemary, who was patiently explaining braiding all over again to the boys in Topaz dorm.

"It must have been serious," said Zara, searching Lily's face for clues.

"Oh my gosh! Are you in trouble?" Phoebe gasped.

Skye overheard and snorted with laughter. "Lily in trouble? As if! Lily's scared of her own shadow!"

"No, she's not!" Feather stamped a hoof furiously. "Leave Lily alone, Skye!" A pink spark flickered in the corner of Lily's eye, and she caught the scent of something sweet.

39

"Or what?" Skye laughed.

"Or . . . or I'll get really angry!" Feather glared at her, even though Lily could see her body trembling with nerves.

Skye grinned. "Ooh, I'm so scared, Feather!" she teased.

"Shh! Ms. Rosemary's coming," said Firefly quickly. "Skye, you haven't finished braiding my mane!"

"What's going on here?" Ms. Rosemary said, walking over.

No one said anything.

"Hmm," said Ms. Rosemary, looking around at all of them. "Well, by the look of these braids, none of you should be standing chitchatting. You've got some practicing to do unless you want me to keep you for an extra braiding class at lunchtime."

There were sounds of alarm and everyone moved quickly away. Lily hugged Feather, her black hair mingling with Feather's violet-yellow-and-blue mane.

"Thank you for standing up for me," she whispered.

"It was nothing," mumbled Feather.

But Lily knew exactly how much courage it had taken, and she felt a rush of love for her loyal unicorn. "You're the best, Feather. I'm so glad I was paired with you."

Feather whickered softly and rubbed her head against Lily's chest.

CHAPTER 4

At dinnertime, Lily found out she was not the only one with family who'd been affected by a purple tornado. Reports had come in of other tornadoes that had struck, leaving a trail of damage and a thick layer of purple dust behind.

"My aunt on the east coast lost every tree in her garden," Johan from Topaz dorm announced, twirling a strand of spaghetti around his fork. "One tree landed across her front door. The neighbors had to rescue her."

"My dad was taking a bath when the roof blew right off our house," said Spike. "He said he'd never

grabbed a towel so quickly!" There was a lot of laughter. Spike grinned and ran a hand through his red hair. "It's true," he added. "And my granny was staying over, and her false teeth ended up in the paddock with Franny, the donkey. Mom only just stopped Franny from eating them."

Lily giggled. Sometimes she didn't know who told taller tales—Spike or Phoebe.

"Hmm. I wonder what's causing all these tornadoes." Zara pulled a tiny notebook and pencil from her pocket. She wrote the date at the top of a new page. "It's extremely unusual to have so many all at once. I think we should make notes of where the tornadoes happened and at what time."

"Wow, I feel so much safer now that Detective Zara is on the case," said Skye sarcastically, rolling her eyes at Amber.

Zara glared at Skye. "My uncle actually is a

detective and I've been learning lots of skills from him."

"My uncle actually is a detective," Skye mimicked, sounding remarkably like Zara. "Get over yourself, Zara. The tornadoes are caused by freak weather. The fact there are so many is just a coincidence."

Lily wished she could be like Zara and shrug off Skye's teasing. "Laugh all you want, Skye," Zara said. "But my uncle says a good detective should always question coincidences."

"What if these tornadoes are caused by dark magic and they're part of an evil plot to take over the island?" said Phoebe, her eyes widening. "It could be Ms. Primrose or Ms. Willow again!"

"No, it couldn't. They're both in prison," Zara pointed out.

"But it could be someone else! It's a mystery!" said Aisha in excitement.

"Oh, puh-lease!" scoffed Skye. "It's just a few tornadoes caused by bad weather. You're all so silly!"

Zara turned her back to Skye. "It *could* just be bad weather," she said to Aisha, Phoebe, and Lily. "But I think there may be more to it. I wonder if there's a pattern to these tornadoes?"

Lily had a thought—could the magic map help them? Maybe it would now show the damaged buildings and trees, and if they looked at it, they might be able to see if there was a pattern to where the tornadoes were hitting. She was going to suggest it to the others, when she hesitated. What if they went to the map and there wasn't any damage marked on it? She'd look really stupid. *Someone else will probably think about checking the map,* she thought. So she stayed quiet.

Everyone continued to argue about whether

the tornadoes were part of an evil plan or just freak weather. It began to make Lily's head hurt. Quietly, she left the table and ran to the stables. Feather was in her stall picking at a net of hay. She left it immediately, coming over to softly nuzzle Lily's hands.

"Lily, is everything all right?"

"Yes," said Lily, rubbing her forehead. "The others are arguing about all the purple tornadoes that have been hitting the island, so I thought I'd come and talk to you instead."

Feather rubbed her muzzle against Lily. "I'm glad you did. I always like seeing you." Shc blinked at her. "It makes me feel warm inside."

Lily put an arm around her neck. "I feel like that too. I've never had a best friend before, Feather. I . . ." She hesitated and then decided to say what she wanted to, even if it was a bit embarrassing. "I feel like I have one now."

"Me?" asked Feather.

Despite her embarrassment, Lily laughed. "Of course you!" Feather gave a happy sigh. Lily rested her cheek on her neck. For a few moments, they just stood there in contented silence.

"I wish we could do something to stop the tornadoes," Lily said. "They sound awful. What if one comes to the school?" She thought of the beautiful building and its grounds being wrecked. It would be horrible.

"Do you think one might actually come here?" asked Feather anxiously.

"I'm not sure. Zara thinks there might be a pattern. Maybe we would be able to see one if we looked at the magic map." She glanced at Feather, wondering what she would think.

"That's a great idea!" said Feather. "Why don't you go look?"

Lily nodded, feeling pleased. "It's a bit late now. I'll go tomorrow. I might even ask Aisha, Zara, and Phoebe to come with me." Being with Feather made her feel so much braver. *Yes,* she told herself firmly. *Tomorrow I'll ask the others to come and look at the magic map with me, and we'll see if we can figure out what's going on . . . and if the academy's in danger!*

CHAPTER 5

The next morning, Lily didn't feel so confident about asking the others if they wanted to look at the map with her.

Maybe I should go on my own first, she decided at breakfast as she ate her cereal. *That way, if nothing is showing on the map, I won't feel silly.*

She hung back as Zara, Aisha, and Phoebe went to the dorm to get ready for Geography with Ms. Rivers, and then she headed for the hall. As she walked through the entrance hall she saw Skye, Amber, and Lorna, another girl from Opal

dorm, huddled around a statue of a rearing unicorn.

"Go on, I dare you to do it!" hissed Skye.

Lorna giggled as she quickly scrambled onto the unicorn's back. She pulled a frilly pink scarf from her pocket and hooked it over the unicorn's head, pulling it until it sat over one ear. "What do you think?" she called down to Skye and Amber.

Rocking with laughter, Skye and Amber gave Lorna a thumbs-up.

Lily stared in shock. How could they look so happy, and play silly dares, when there were tornadoes around the island and the school itself might be in danger?

"Squeak, squeak! Look, it's little Lily Mouse!" said Skye, noticing her. "Is that *your* scarf on that statue, Lily Mouse?" She hooted with laughter.

Amber and Lorna joined in. "Squeak, squeak, squeak!" They giggled.

Lily ran past them and didn't stop running until she reached the main hall. The big double doors were slightly open. She glanced around. She wasn't planning to use the map—she just wanted to look at it. But what if a teacher found her near it and she got in trouble just for being there without permission?

She made up her mind. It was worth the risk.

Slipping through the doors, she hurried toward the map. The magical force field buzzed softly as if to warn her away. Lily took a deep breath, and the butterflies behind her rib cage slowed down. Would the force field let her get close enough for a good look? She walked toward the

map, and as she approached, there was a soft *pop* and the humming stopped. A grin spread across Lily's face.

"Thanks," she whispered to the map. It was as though it was happy she was there—maybe it even wanted her to help.

The map was even more incredible close up. The glass-and-marble model of the school looked so real that, peering through a tiny window, Lily almost expected to see herself inside the building! She looked to the east, to her village. She could see the ruined houses, and for a moment, it took her breath away. *How awful for everyone!* Her eyes searched the map, following the path of the purple tornadoes—the fallen trees and damaged buildings. The tornadoes seemed to have zigzagged across the island from the east coast to the west and back again. She traced the pattern with her eyes. If it continued in the same way, then the tornadoes would definitely reach the school!

Lily jumped as she heard voices outside the doors. Someone was coming! If she was discovered, she could get in trouble. She had to hide!

She ran across the hall, scrambled onto the stage, and ducked behind the stage curtains just as Ms. Mallow, the new school nurse, came in with Ms. Rivers, the teacher who taught both

Geography and Culture. Ms. Mallow walked toward the map. Lily held her breath, letting it out quietly when she heard the soft hum of the force field again. Ms. Mallow shook her head. "Strange, I was sure the force field had stopped working for a moment, but it seems all right. I must have imagined it."

"It was smart to check, with everything that's happening," said Ms. Rivers. "Now, where's that book I said I'd lend you?" She walked up the steps onto the stage and went to the piano.

Lily froze, hardly daring to breathe as Ms. Rivers came within touching distance of her.

"Here it is." Lily heard Ms. Rivers walk back to the floor. She peeked out from behind the curtain. "Are you sure that I can't persuade you to come to the meeting Ms. Nettles is holding at lunchtime, Ms. Mallow?"

"No. She has given me special permission to get

on with my work," said Ms. Mallow. "I'm making a large batch of cough syrup. You know how it is at the start of winter semester. The students spread their germs with the speed of a forest fire. And if these tornadoes are being caused by bad magic, we're going to need the students to stay strong and healthy."

Ms. Rivers nodded, worry lines creasing her face. "It does seem like these tornadoes might be part of an evil plan. No one has ever heard of a purple tornado on the island before, let alone lots of them."

"But who would create such terrible things?" asked Ms. Mallow.

Ms. Rivers sounded grave. "Someone who uses dark magic. Someone who wants to harm our island, and the people and unicorns who live on it."

Ms. Rivers and Ms. Mallow left the hall.

Lily's heart was thumping hard. Still trembling, she came out from behind the curtain, crept out of the hall, and raced up to the dorm. She had to tell the others what she'd seen and overheard!

The girls were getting ready, sorting out their pencil cases and bags. As Lily burst in, they looked around.

"I know something about the tornadoes!" she exclaimed, her usual shyness overcome by the urge to tell them what she'd discovered.

Everyone gaped at her. The words continued to tumble from her mouth as she described how she'd gone to look at the map and overheard the teachers talking.

"The damage is all there on the map and the pattern is very clear," she finished breathlessly. "The tornadoes are crisscrossing up the island from east to west and back again. Ms. Rivers thinks someone might have used dark magic to create them. Someone who wants to harm the island!"

"But that's terrible!" exclaimed Phoebe.

"Who would want to harm the island?" asked Aisha.

"Ms. Rivers didn't seem to know," said Lily.

"I'll write to my uncle, the detective, and see if he knows of any likely suspects," said Zara. She pulled out her notebook and scribbled a note to herself.

"The worst thing is that when I was looking at the map, I could see that if the tornadoes keep going in this pattern, they're going to reach the academy," Lily said.

"What! The school could be

destroyed and our unicorns might be hurt?" cried Phoebe.

Lily nodded anxiously.

"But surely the teachers will stop the tornadoes in time, won't they?" said Aisha.

Lily gulped. "What if they can't?"

There was a moment's silence as they all looked at each other.

"We've got to solve this mystery!" Zara declared. "Amethyst dorm, we're going to find out who created these tornadoes, and we're going to stop them!"

CHAPTER 6

Lily and the others were settling into their seats
for their Geography lesson, when the door opened
and Ms. Tulip hurried in. She taught Riding, and
Lily loved her cross-country lessons.

"Girls! Boys!" She clapped her hands. "Ms.
Rivers has sent me to tell you there will be no
Geography class today. There have been reports
of another tornado sweeping through one of
the villages south of the academy. The damage
is very bad, and Ms. Nettles wants all students
and their unicorns to ride there to help with the
cleanup. Put your books away and go to the

stables. You will be out all day—a packed lunch will be provided for you."

She left the room, and everyone began to talk in excitement as they put their books away. Zara turned to the others in Amethyst dorm.

"This is our chance! We might find some clues in the damaged village that will help us work out what's going on!"

It was a cold winter morning. The academy buildings were covered with a layer of glittering frost, and Sparkle Lake glowed like a rainbow in the pale winter sunlight. The students cantered their unicorns in a line out of the grounds and toward the damaged village. Everyone carried a backpack containing an emergency repair kit of string, nails, and a hammer as well as their lunch.

"I hope we're able to help," Feather said as her hooves pounded the hard ground.

"Me too," said Lily, wrapping her hands in Feather's mane for warmth. "We must be nearly there," she added. The path they were on was covered with a fine layer of purple dust. As they got closer to the village, Lily gasped. There was so much damage! Windows were smashed, doors and roofs were missing, and nothing was where it should be.

Ms. Rivers pulled up, waving at the students.
"Spread out," she said. "Help as many people
and animals as you can, but do not put yourself in
any danger. If you can't solve the problem, then
find a teacher and ask for help!"

"Where shall we start?" asked Feather. Her ears
twisted. "Listen!" she exclaimed. "Can you hear
that?"

Lily heard it too, the whine of an animal—a dog, maybe. "It's coming from over there," she said, pointing to a sheet of metal roofing lying on the ground next to a smashed-up barn. "Something's trapped underneath."

Feather picked her way over, treading a careful path through broken tiles and bricks. Lily jumped from her back, and using both hands, she tried to lift the metal up.

"It's really heavy!" she puffed. Flexing her fingers, she heaved with all her might. With a screeching sound, the metal moved a tiny bit. Through the gap, Lily felt the tickle of breath on her hands and heard the whining get louder. She bit her lip, holding the metal sheet steady but unable to lift it any higher. Feather used her muzzle to try to help, but it only moved a few centimeters.

"Move, metal! Move!" Feather said, stamping

a hoof in frustration. Pink sparks suddenly flew up, and Lily noticed the strong smell of burnt sugar.

Lily gasped. "Feather! What's happening?"

Feather didn't speak. She was staring at the metal sheet. It started to lift into the air! Lily watched openmouthed as it slowly floated to a patch of nettles and came down to rest. With a grateful *woof,* the dog who had been trapped under it bolted away.

"Feather! You've found your magic!" Lily cried.

"I have!" said Feather, sounding equally surprised. "I've got moving magic, Lily. Just like my grampy."

Aisha, Zara, and Phoebe came running over.

"Did Feather just move that metal sheet by magic?" Zara demanded.

"I did! I did!" Feather whinnied excitedly. "I've got moving magic!"

"Bravo, Feather, you superstar!" Phoebe said. "Everyone!" she shouted. "Feather's found her magic and it's amazing!"

Feather was the first unicorn in their class to get her magic. The nearby students crowded around, all wanting to congratulate her. Lily shyly stood to one side as Feather seemed to glow with the praise.

"Let's see you move something again!" said Silver.

"Okay. Watch me move that chimney," said Feather, stamping a hoof and making a fallen chimney rise into the air. Feather turned it the right way up and set it down by the side of the house it had fallen from. Everyone cheered.

Feather looked delighted. "Now watch me lift up that cart."

"Shouldn't you rest first?" asked Lily anxiously. Her mom had warned her that when unicorns first started using their magic, they usually found it very draining.

"I'm perfectly fine, thanks," said Feather.

"You probably shouldn't do too much at first," said Aisha in concern.

"Yes, your magic's amazing, Feather, but you don't want to overdo it. We should all do more cleaning," said Zara. "You can show us more later when we're back at school."

The rest of the students nodded and hurried off, except for Skye and Amber.

"Do something else!" Skye called.

"Yeah, let's see what else you can move!" said Amber.

Feather looked pleased. "All right."

"No, Feather, you'll tire yourself out," said Lily.

Feather ignored her and faced the upside-down cart. She stamped her hoof. "Move, cart!" With a faint hiss, a lone pink spark rose from the ground and then faded. The cart trembled and its wheels spun.

Skye and Amber giggled.

"I wouldn't call that amazing," said Skye.

"Move," said Feather, her cheeks wobbling with determination. She stamped a hoof again, and this time, two sparks flew up and a barrel lying near the cart rose into the air.

"Eek!" Amber shrieked, pulling Skye down just in time as the barrel swept over their heads and then came crashing down next to them, breaking into smithereens.

Skye sat up, her eyes wide. "Feather, you could have hurt us! Your moving magic isn't amazing!"

She pointed at the broken barrel. "And you're not good at it!"

Feather's face fell, and she glanced hopefully at Lily.

Lily knew that she should defend Feather, but she was too scared of what Skye might say if she did, and the words got tangled on her tongue.

Skye and Amber turned and left.

"Ignore them, Feather!" Lily said quickly. "Your magic is great." Her heart sank as she saw the hurt look on her unicorn's face. She knew she'd let Feather down.

"Feather?" she said. But Feather didn't answer.

CHAPTER 7

Lily and Feather were silent as they rode back to school. Lily felt awful. Why hadn't she defended Feather to Skye?

Because you're a coward, a voice whispered in her head. *If you can't even stand up for your own unicorn, you'll never be brave enough to be a guardian!*

When they got back to the stables, Lily fluffed up the fresh straw in Feather's stall and brought her an extra-large helping of sky berries, the magical fruit that helped bring back a unicorn's magic. She acted as though everything was fine, hoping that if

she pretended things were normal between her and Feather, they would be.

"Lots of yummy sky berries. You'll feel stronger after eating these," said Lily, tipping the berries into Feather's manger.

"Thanks," Feather muttered.

Lily went to the door and then hesitated. Part of her just wanted to leave the stable, to say goodnight and hurry inside. But she couldn't keep pretending that everything was okay when she knew that it wasn't. Gathering her courage, she forced herself to speak. "Feather, I'm so sorry," she said. "I should have stood up to Skye. I wanted to. I really did. But I couldn't get my words out."

Feather nodded stiffly. "Okay . . . Well, thanks for apologizing but I think I'll rest now. I am tired," she said, turning her back to Lily.

"See you tomorrow," Lily whispered unhappily as she left the stable.

She was walking slowly back to the academy when someone ran up behind her.

"Lily, wait," said Aisha, slipping her arm through Lily's. "I couldn't help overhearing some of the stuff back there in the stable with Feather. Are you all right?"

"Not really. I think I've messed things up between Feather and me," said Lily sadly.

"Don't worry, I'm sure it can be fixed," Aisha said. She thought for a moment. "I know! Why don't you go to the stables early tomorrow and offer to help Feather practice her magic? I practice playing my flute every day. I bet Feather will get really good at using her moving magic once she's practiced a bit more, and she'll be happy if you offer to help her."

That makes sense. It's like my paper folding, thought Lily. She hadn't been good at it at first, but with lots of practice, her paper models were now pretty

good. "That's a great idea. Thanks, Aisha. I'll go see Feather first thing and ask if she wants my help."

"I bet she'll say yes!" said Aisha. "And everything will be okay again!" The two girls shared a hopeful smile.

★

Lily woke up early the following morning, before the sun started to rise. Quietly, she dressed in the dark room. She took a flashlight from her drawer, picked up the paper unicorn she had made before she went to bed, and slipped outside to the stables. The icy January air stung her cheeks as she ran along the path.

When she got to the stables, she found Feather asleep, curled up in the straw, her nostrils quivering and her long eyelashes fluttering on her face. Lily stood for a moment, her heart swelling with love.

I won't let you down again, Feather. I'll be braver from now on. I'll stand up for you, no matter how scared I am, Lily silently promised.

Feather woke suddenly, her eyes snapping open. She jumped up. "Lily! What are you doing here so early?"

"I wanted to say sorry again. I'm going to stand up for you in the future and not let anyone put you down—ever!" Lily said in a rush. "Look, I made you this and I came to help you practice your magic—if you want my help. . . ." She

stopped, suddenly shy. Timidly, she placed the paper unicorn on Feather's manger.

"Did you really make this?" Feather asked, gently touching the delicate unicorn with her nose. "That's amazing, Lily."

"It was nothing," said Lily, and then stopped herself. "Actually, it wasn't nothing. It was really hard, and I had to practice for ages before I got it right. But I did it and now I want you to have it."

Feather studied her for a moment. "Thank you. Yesterday was awful. I felt really sad when you didn't stand up for me. But I thought about it last night and I realized how hard it must have been for you when Skye was being mean. I felt glad you'd said sorry afterward, and I wish I'd said something nicer back." She pushed her head against Lily. "I couldn't go to sleep. I just wanted us to make up. I don't want anything to come between us ever again."

"Me neither," said Lily. "I really *am* sorry, and I promise I will always be there for you from now on."

"And I'll be there for you," Feather said.

Lily hugged Feather tightly.

"So do you want to practice some magic?" Lily asked.

Feather nodded eagerly. She started by moving small things, a hoof pick, a grooming brush, then a comb, lifting them up and bringing them to Lily. After a while, she tried bigger things like a bucket, empty at first and then filled with water. She was soon very good at it. Then Feather started to have some fun.

"Is that Skye's hoodie?" Lily giggled as Feather hung the forgotten hoodie near the roof. "Feather, that's Dynamo's rug! Put it back!" she added as Feather draped a striped orange rug across an empty stall to make a tent. Feather was decorating

the clock hands with ribbons she'd moved from the storeroom, when Aisha came in, making Lily and her both jump.

"Eek! You scared me! I usually hear you humming before you arrive," said Lily, giggling.

"I can hum if you want. I just didn't want to wake anyone up," said Aisha with a grin. "I saw you'd gone from the dorm and thought I'd find you here. Are you coming in for breakfast?"

"I could use my magic and you could both have breakfast here," said Feather, her eyes shining. "We could get Silver and have a picnic in the barn next to the stables. What would you like to eat?"

"Ooh, that'd be fun. I'll have scrambled eggs, toast, and apple juice, please," said Aisha.

"That sounds nice. Can I have the same?" Lily asked.

Aisha went to get Silver, and they all made their

way to the center of the barn. While Lily and Aisha put out some hay bales to sit on, Feather used her moving magic to bring them food from the kitchen and sky berries from the feed room.

"Wow, look!" Aisha giggled as plates of scrambled eggs, a rack of toast, a jug of apple juice, glasses, and silverware floated through the open barn door, followed by two buckets of sky berries.

Silver whinnied. "I wish I had moving magic!"

"Feather, you're just showing off now!" Lily said with a grin as Feather made a knife and fork bow to each other before dancing.

"Never!" Feather said, wide-eyed as she made the spoons somersault.

"This is the best way to have breakfast," said Aisha.

Lily looked at Aisha, Silver, and Feather and sighed with contentment. For the first time since starting at Unicorn Academy, she actually felt as if she really and truly belonged there.

They were just finishing when they heard the

drum of hooves on hard winter ground. "What's that?" said Silver.

They went to the barn door. A group of unicorns and adult riders were galloping away from the stables across the school grounds.

"That's the teachers!" exclaimed Lily. "Where are they going?"

"It must be something urgent," said Aisha.

"Maybe it's something to do with the tornadoes?" said Feather anxiously.

Aisha grabbed Lily's hand. "Quick, let's go find out what's happening. See you later, Silver!"

Lily blew Feather a kiss, and then she and Aisha raced back to school.

CHAPTER 8

The academy was quiet. The halls were unusually empty. Lily and Aisha went looking for Zara and Phoebe and found them in the lounge, huddled beside a roaring fire. Zara was writing furiously in her notebook, and Phoebe was pacing up and down.

"What's happened?" asked Aisha.

"Chaos!" said Phoebe with a dramatic sweep of her arm. "Our beautiful island is being destroyed by purple tornadoes. They're whirling across the land, destroying everything in their path!"

"Enough with the drama, Phoebe," said Zara.

Pushing her hair behind her ears, she explained. "There were more purple tornadoes last night, closer to the school. The teachers have gone to check it out. I overheard Ms. Nettles talking about it with Ms. Rosemary. They also think it's someone using dark magic."

"But why didn't they take us with them to help clean up?" said Aisha.

"They're worried that another tornado will hit nearby while they're out, and they thought we'd be safer here at school."

Lily caught her breath. "But what if a tornado hits the academy?" They all looked at her. She rushed on. "I told you what I'd seen on the map. It looked like the tornadoes are zigzagging across the island, and if they keep going, they'll reach the school! The teachers must not have realized this!"

"Let's go check!" cried Zara.

They raced to the hall. The force field protecting the map stopped humming and let them through right away.

It's as if it wants us to help, Lily thought again. She hurried closer, and her heart sank as she saw how damaged the map was now.

"You're right, Lily!" Zara breathed, pointing. "If the tornadoes keep happening, it looks like one will hit the school today!"

"What should we do?" Aisha's eyes were huge. "The teachers are all gone!"

"We need to warn everyone," said Zara. "There's still time for us to get out of the way."

"But what about the academy?" Lily couldn't bear the thought of it being smashed to pieces. "There has to be a way we can save it!"

"There's nothing we can do," said Phoebe. "None of our unicorns have magic yet, except Feather."

Feather! A plan sprang into Lily's brain. She bit her lip. Should she say it out loud? Would her friends just laugh at her? She shoved her fears down. She'd decided she was going to speak up from now on and she would start right away!

"Feather might be able to help!" she burst out. "She could try to use her moving magic to steer the tornado away from the school and push it out to the ocean."

"Oh yes!" Phoebe cried, clasping her hands, and Aisha nodded.

Zara frowned. "Lily, I really don't mean this to sound mean, but is Feather's magic strong enough to do something like that yet?"

"She was awesome this morning!" said Aisha. "She was moving whatever she wanted."

Lily shot her a grateful look. "Look, it may not work," she said to Zara. "I can't promise she'll be able to do it. But I believe in her, and right now

we don't have any other plans. This might be our only hope! We have to try!"

"Okay," said Zara, taking command. "If you believe Feather can do it, then I believe it too, Lily." Lily glowed inside. "Let's call a meeting of the whole school in the stables, and Lily can tell everyone what the plan is."

Lily's stomach sank. It was one thing speaking in front of her friends, but the whole school? "Oh no," she whispered, shaking her head. "I can't speak in front of everyone.

I just can't. Could you please do that part, Zara?"

"If you're sure?" Zara looked happy when Lily nodded. "Okay, I'll do that. You go tell Feather what's happening, and we'll get everyone to the stables! Come on! There isn't a moment to waste!"

As Lily ran to the stables, she felt a curl of panic inside. Should she have asked Feather before offering her help? But there hadn't been time. She ran faster.

"Lily, what is it?" Feather left her hay as Lily ran into her stall.

Panting for breath, Lily explained.

For a moment, Feather was silent. Then she asked quietly, "Do you think I can do this, Lily? Do you really believe my magic is strong enough?"

Lily didn't hesitate. "Yes. I do. You can help save the school, Feather. I know it."

Feather took a deep breath. "Then I'll try."

"I'll be with you the whole time." Lily said. "And if anyone dares to say anything mean, they'll have me to deal with!"

★

The students gathered in the stable yard, shouting and calling out, wanting to know what was going on. Zara stood on a mounting block and addressed them. "Listen up, everyone," she called, clapping her hands like a teacher. "This is an emergency."

She quickly explained about the tornado and how Feather was going to try to stop it. She'd barely finished speaking when Skye interrupted.

"As if that will work," she scoffed. "Feather's magic isn't strong enough to move a cart, let alone a tornado!"

"Oh yes it is!" cried Lily. Feather gave her a grateful look. "Feather was tired yesterday because she'd only just got her magic, but she's been practicing this morning and she's really good at using it now. So you can just . . . just *be quiet*, Skye!"

There were a number of gasps. Skye gaped, lost for words for once. Feather nuzzled Lily's shoulder, and Lily felt a happy glow.

"Lily's right," called Aisha. "Feather can do this."

Silver whinnied in support and the rest of the unicorns joined in. Lily felt a rush of triumph. "Then what are we waiting for?" she shouted, courage rushing through her as she saw the look of love that Feather was giving her. "Let's save the school!"

CHAPTER 9

As everyone cleared a space around Feather, Aisha let out a squeal. "Lily, your hair! You've bonded with Feather."

Lily lifted the violet-yellow-and-blue strand in her black hair and stared at it in wonder.

Feather nuzzled her face against Lily's.

"Three cheers for Lily and Feather! The first partners at Unicorn Academy to find their magic and bond! Hip, hip, hooray!" Phoebe cried.

As the cheering died away, the sky suddenly

90

darkened and a breeze sprang up from nowhere. Empty buckets clattered across the yard.

"It's the tornado!" said Zara. "It's coming! Into the stables, everyone!"

Lily took a deep breath as the others started hurrying inside. "This is it, Feather."

Feather lifted her head. "I'm going to save the academy, Lily!"

Lily placed a hand on her neck. "And I'm going to be right here with you."

The wind grew stronger, tossing Lily's hair and Feather's mane around. There was a roaring noise that quickly grew louder. In the distance, Lily saw a blur of purple coming across the grounds toward the school buildings. The trees began to bend, their branches whipping back and forth. Twigs snapped off and flew in the air. Lily, standing shoulder to shoulder with

Feather, ducked as bits of trees and bushes whirled past her and the wind screamed in her ears.

The tornado continued to grow, towering in the air as it headed toward the academy. It glittered dully as it spun closer, leaving purple dust on the grounds and Sparkle Lake. The stench of bad magic hung in the air. It tickled the back of Lily's throat, making her cough and her eyes water.

Feather, her gaze fixed on the tornado, muttered, "I can do this."

"You can!" Lily said hoarsely. "I know you can!" She wiped her eyes. The tornado was so close—any minute now it would hit them. . . . Lily blinked. The tornado looked like it was

hesitating. Was it turning away from the school? No, it was definitely moving, slowly changing course, heading toward the mountains and out to the ocean. "It's working!" she cried, stroking Feather's neck. "Don't give up, Feather."

"Stay beside me, Lily," Feather panted. "Keep talking to me. It helps."

"I'm not going anywhere." Lily continued to stroke Feather's neck as she focused her magic to move the tornado. "I know you're strong enough to do this." The tornado moved even farther away. "It's almost gone!" she exclaimed. "Keep going, Feather."

The towering purple tornado rose over the highest mountain peak, wobbling as it moved away. Then, suddenly, a man's voice boomed from the sky. His words were strong at first, but faded away as the tornado spun out to sea. "You think you can stop me, but you can't. I will . . ."

His voice disappeared into the howling wind.

Feather's body trembled and her legs sagged.

"You did it, Feather!" Lily cried.

Zara, Phoebe, and Aisha ran out of the stables.

"Did you hear that man's voice?" asked Zara, pulling out her notebook. "What did it say? 'You think you can stop me, but you can't. . . .' What else did he say?"

Everyone shook their heads. No one had heard the rest of the words.

"I have no idea what this means," said Zara, her mouth set in a determined line, "but at least we know now that the person behind these tornadoes is a man. I'm going to find out more!"

"We'll all help, won't we?" said Aisha. "If we don't find out who did this, they could do it again! Raise your hand if you're in."

Lily, Zara, Phoebe, and Aisha all raised their hands.

"Amethyst dorm will find the culprit!" chanted Phoebe. "Amethyst dorm is the best!"

Everyone else started to spill out of the stables. At the same moment, Lily heard the sound of beating hooves.

"It's the teachers!" she said, spinning around to look.

Ms. Nettles, closely followed by the rest of the staff, galloped up.

"Is everyone all right?" Ms. Nettles demanded. "What happened? We saw the tornado heading toward the school, and we came back as fast as we could. Where did it go?"

All eyes turned to Lily and Feather, and Lily felt her face flood with color. Feather nodded as if to say, "You can do this." Lily took a deep breath, but as she started to speak, Skye stepped forward.

"We were all indoors when—"

"Be quiet, Skye," said Zara.

"Let Lily and Feather speak if they want to! It's their story," Aisha said.

Lily smiled gratefully at her new friends. She paused for another moment, then told the story.

Ms. Nettles listened carefully as Lily retold their adventures, from tracking the storm on the magic map to Feather stopping it.

"Thank you for saving the academy, Feather, and to you, Lily, for encouraging her and standing with her. If you hadn't been there for her, her magic wouldn't have been strong enough. It's the bond between a unicorn and their partner that gives the unicorn's magic added power and strength," said Ms. Nettles. "I'm delighted you have bonded and discovered Feather's magic. I told you the other day that guardians all have different strengths. But the one quality all guardians share is bravery, and you have certainly shown that today."

"I—I'm not brave," stammered Lily.

Ms. Nettles's eyes seemed to see right inside her. "You are, my dear. Bravery is not about who shouts the loudest. It's about doing what you know is right even when that's difficult and you feel scared. You and Feather are truly brave, Lily, and I know you will be wonderful guardians of our island." She smiled at them and then looked around at everyone else. "Well, this has certainly been an exciting start to the year! Now everyone please settle your unicorns back in the stalls. Then go to the hall, where I'll ask the cook to provide hot chocolate and cookies."

"But, Ms. Nettles, what about the person we heard?" said Zara. "Are you going to try to find out who he is?"

"Yes, he may strike again!" exclaimed Phoebe.

Ms. Nettles looked at them over the top of her glasses. "I understand your concern, girls, but you don't need to worry. The teachers and I will deal with it from now on." She turned and rode away, leaving Zara staring after her.

"We'll see about that," she muttered. "This is a mystery and I'm going to help solve it."

"We all are!" said Phoebe, linking arms with her.

"We definitely will. But first, cookies and hot chocolate sound good, don't they, Lily?" said Aisha.

Lily grinned at her dorm. "Oh yes!"

They all took their unicorns back to their stalls.

"You were amazing," said Lily, stroking Feather's face.

"You were amazing too," said Feather, nuzzling her. "Thank you for standing up for me when Skye was being mean."

Lily hugged her. "I promise I'll always be here

for you. I'm going to speak up when I need to. After today, I'm not scared of anyone."

Feather whickered softly. "Me neither. We've always got each other. That's all that matters."

"It really is," said Lily, kissing her on the neck.

Feather's eyes sparkled. "But now it's time to join your friends for hot chocolate and cookies. Hold on tight, Lily." She stamped her hoof, and Lily gasped as she suddenly found herself on Feather's back, gliding out of the stables and across the grass to the school.

"Feather!" she shrieked. "What are you doing?"

"Having fun with my magic, Lily!" Feather whinnied back. "Having fun!"

An inspector is coming to Unicorn Academy! Can Phoebe and Shimmer make sure the school passes the inspection?

Read on for a peek at the next book in the Unicorn Academy Nature Magic series!

"You'll never guess what I just saw!" Phoebe exclaimed, bursting into Amethyst dorm. Her eyes sparkled with excitement. "Well?" she said, looking around eagerly at her dorm mates—Zara, Lily, and Aisha. "Come on, guess!"

"No time. You can tell us later," said Zara, pulling her hoodie over her dark brown hair.

"Yes, hurry up now, Phoebe, or we'll be late for the cross-country ride with Ms. Tulip," said Lily. Aisha didn't say anything. She was too busy looking for something under her bed.

"But this is important!" Phoebe said. She wanted

her friends to feel the same excitement she did. "Okay, so this is what happened," she said, going into what Zara called her storytelling mode. "I was coming back from breakfast, just walking in the hall, minding my own business, when I saw Ms. Rosemary and Ms. Rivers whispering together outside Ms. Nettles's office. They left, and I heard Ms. Nettles making a weird noise, so I sneaked a look around the door, and guess what?" Phoebe paused dramatically as she remembered what she had seen in the headteacher's office. "Ms. Nettles was really upset!"

Her friends continued to get ready, not looking up.

"She was crying!" Phoebe said, to get their attention. "Loudly, with lots of tears. Well, what do you think about that?"

"Found it!" Aisha crawled out from under her bed. She was clutching a purple hoodie. "Who was sighing?"

"Ms. Nettles was *crying*," said Phoebe, looking around at her friends. "Don't you think that is super weird? Headteachers don't cry. Something must be going on!"

"Was Ms. Nettles really crying, Phoebe?" Zara said, raising her eyebrows. "Or are you just exaggerating like usual?"

"No! I'm not!" Phoebe insisted. "I promise, Ms. Nettles was a hundred percent crying. She blew her nose and it sounded as loud as an elephant trumpeting!"

"Oh, I hope she's okay," said Lily, looking concerned.

Zara frowned. "I'm sure she is. There's probably a simple reason. She could have been tearing up because her allergies came back."

Phoebe rolled her eyes. "You are *so* boring, Zara!"

"Not boring, just logical," said Zara with a grin. "Seriously, there's been enough drama happening here without having to make stuff up, Phoebe. Purple tornadoes sweeping across the island, the school almost being destroyed, a strange voice in the tornado saying they're not going to be stopped . . ."

"Aha! But maybe those things have something to do with Ms. Nettles's crying," said Phoebe. "Maybe something else has happened and she's found out about it! Maybe there's been another tornado or something even"—she paused dramatically—"*worse!*"

"Or maybe Ms. Nettles just has allergies," said

Zara again. "It is springtime after all, and there's a lot of pollen in the air."

Lily turned to Phoebe. "Come on, Phoebe. We really have to go. We'll be in trouble with Ms. Tulip if we're late."

Phoebe sighed. She brushed her long honey-blond hair before braiding it. She loved her three friends in Amethyst dorm, but she sometimes felt they really didn't get her. She liked to make everything seem as exciting as possible, but they seemed to just want to know the facts. How boring was that?

MERMICORNs

Swim into a new series!

MERMICORNs 1

Sparkle Magic

Sudipta Bardhan-Quallen

Mermicorns are part unicorn, part mermaid, and totally magical!

PuRRmaids

Meet your newest feline friends!

PuRRmaids
The Scaredy Cat

1

Sudipta Bardhan-Quallen

rhcbooks.com RHCB

New friends. New adventures.
Find a new series... just for you!

ISADORA MOON

Isadora Moon Goes to School
Harriet Muncaster

For ballerina and fairy and vampire lovers

MAGIC ON THE MAP

Magic on the Map: Let's Mooove!
Courtney Sheinmel & Bianca Turetsky

For adventurers

UNICORN ACADEMY

Unicorn Academy: Sophia and Rainbow
Julie Sykes • Illustrated by Lucy Truman

For unicorn lovers

PUPPY PIRATES

Puppy Pirates: Stowaway!
Erin Soderberg

For dog lovers

PURRMAIDS

Purrmaids: The Scaredy Cat

For mermaid and cat lovers

BALLPARK Mysteries

Ballpark Mysteries Super Special #1: The World Series Curse
David A. Kelly

For sports fans

Purrmaids cover art © Andrew Farley; Purrmaids™ is a registered trademark of KIKIDOODLE LLC and is used under license from KIKIDOODLE LLC. Ballpark Mysteries: cover art © Mark Meyers.

RHCB rhcbooks.com

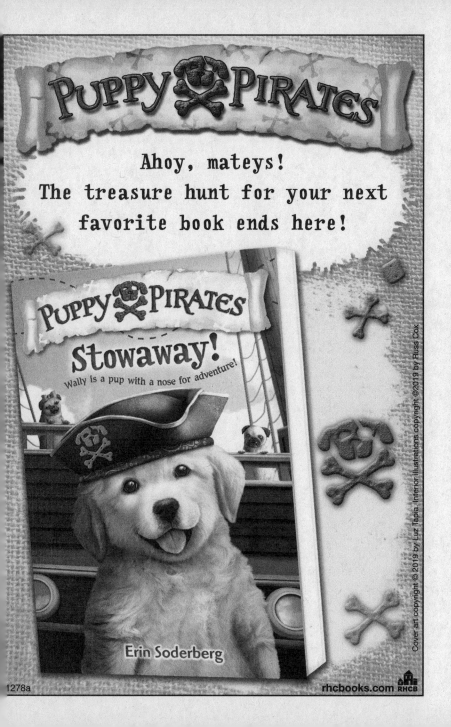

PUPPY 🐾 PIRATES

Ahoy, mateys!
The treasure hunt for your next
favorite book ends here!

PUPPY 🐾 PIRATES

Stowaway!

Wally is a pup with a nose for adventure!

Erin Soderberg

rhcbooks.com RHCB

⌐ Collect all the books in the ⌐
Horse Diaries series!

Every Isadora Moon adventure is totally unique!